LONG-HAIRED CAT-BOY CUB

ETGAR KERET

ILLUSTRATED BY
AVIEL BASIL

LONG-HAIRED CAT-BOY CUB

TRANSLATED BY
SONDRA SILVERSTON

TRIANGLE
SQUARE
books for young readers

SEVEN STORIES

NEW YORK · OAKLAND · LONDON

My dad is a very busy man. In fact, he used to be too busy to see me at all. But not long ago I heard Mom tell him that he has to try to spend more time with me, or else when I grow up, he'll be really, really sorry. Since then, he's been trying hard, but it doesn't always work out.

Like last Tuesday when we were at the zoo and he got a call saying that a businessman from Japan was in his office and wanted to buy two airplanes and a building from him right away. Dad said that it was a once-in-a-lifetime deal. He gave me money for a taxi, and just to be on the safe side, checked twice to make sure I remembered our address. Then he taught me what to say to Mom so she'd be a little less mad at him when I came home alone.

When he was sure that everything was all right and he could count on me, he looked at the clock on his cell phone, gave me a kiss on the nose, right in front of the rhinoceros cage, said, "Promise you'll have fun without me," and left.

I tried very hard to have fun, like I promised Dad,
but I really didn't know how to have fun all by
myself. I walked past all the cages and read what the
signs said about what each animal eats and what it
gets eaten by, about the things it likes and where
it lives in nature. Nothing on the signs said the
animals like to live in cages, but that's what they all
did. Maybe that's why they looked a little sad.

When I started to get hungry, I bought a
hot dog at the stand, and after that, I wanted
to buy some chocolate so the hot dog wouldn't
feel alone in my stomach. But I remembered that
I promised Dad not to buy candy with the money
because he'd have enough trouble with Mom as it was, so I
bought another hot dog for dessert instead. I was very tired after
all those hot dogs. The muscles in my legs hurt, so I looked for a
place to sit down, but all the benches were taken by families. Some
of the families were fat and some were skinny. Some whispered and
some shouted. But they all looked very happy.

The last cage in the zoo was empty. Its door was half open, and the sign at the entrance didn't say anything. So I took a black marker out of my pocket and wrote LONG-HAIRED CAT-BOY CUB on it, and when I went inside, I closed the door behind me. The cage was quiet and pretty nice. There was a tall, crooked tree inside it that gave a lot of shade, and underneath it there was a cool gray rock. I lay down on it for a few minutes and closed my eyes, trying to picture all the animals in the zoo doing what was written on the signs, hunting zebras and climbing trees.

LONG-HAIRED CAT-BOY CUB

And when I opened
my eyes again…

I saw that I was here.

The "here" was a giant airship flying in the sky, and an old turtle, a tiger, and a lazy rhinoceros were in it with me. At the front, right near the steering wheel, a small man with a long beard and soft red hair in his ears was searching for something in an old book, looking very confused. When I asked him politely if I could help, he looked at me and said, "He speaks!"

He came over and shook my hand, just like
Dad told me people do when they close a deal.
Then he said that his name was Habakkuk
and that he was very excited, because he had
never met a long-haired cat-boy cub before.
"You must be a truly rare animal," he said,
"because I've looked you up in all my books,
but couldn't find a thing."

When Habakkuk saw that I wasn't saying anything, he quickly explained to me that he was actually kidnapping animals from zoos and setting them free in their natural habitat. He explained proudly that he'd already set free forty elephants, seven tigers, and one half-blind whale, but I was the first long-haired cat-boy cub he'd ever set free. He'd walked past my cage, and the minute he saw me sleeping there—such a beautiful, noble animal—he read the name on the sign. He looked at me again, and I seemed a little sad to him, so he decided to set me free too.

Habakkuk showed me the special notebooks he kept for each animal on the airship. In the notebooks, he wrote down what the animal eats, where it lives, and most important of all—what it doesn't like. In his elephant notebook, for instance, he wrote that they're happiest when you pet their tongues because that's the only part of their body soft enough for them to feel the petting. The bear likes raw fish, and the hippopotamus really hates getting shampoo in its eyes.

"Everything is written down in my notebooks,"
Habakkuk said sadly, "and only the one for the
long-haired cat-boy cub is empty." I said I
would help and tell him everything I know,
which made him very happy, and on
the first page of his little notebook
he wrote in large blue letters
CAT-BOY CUBS ARE KIND
AND HELPFUL.

FELIS CATULUS HUMANUS

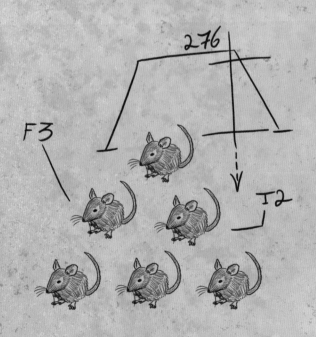

So, while we were setting all the animals free in their natural habitats and saying goodbye to them, I told Habakkuk everything you need to know about long-haired cat-boy cubs. Like, for instance, that they only eat candy, that you're not allowed to wash them with water, and that if you don't play at least one game an hour with them, they might die. I also told him that their favorite games are cards and tag with mice. But you have to be careful, because if they lose too many times, their fur starts to fall out.

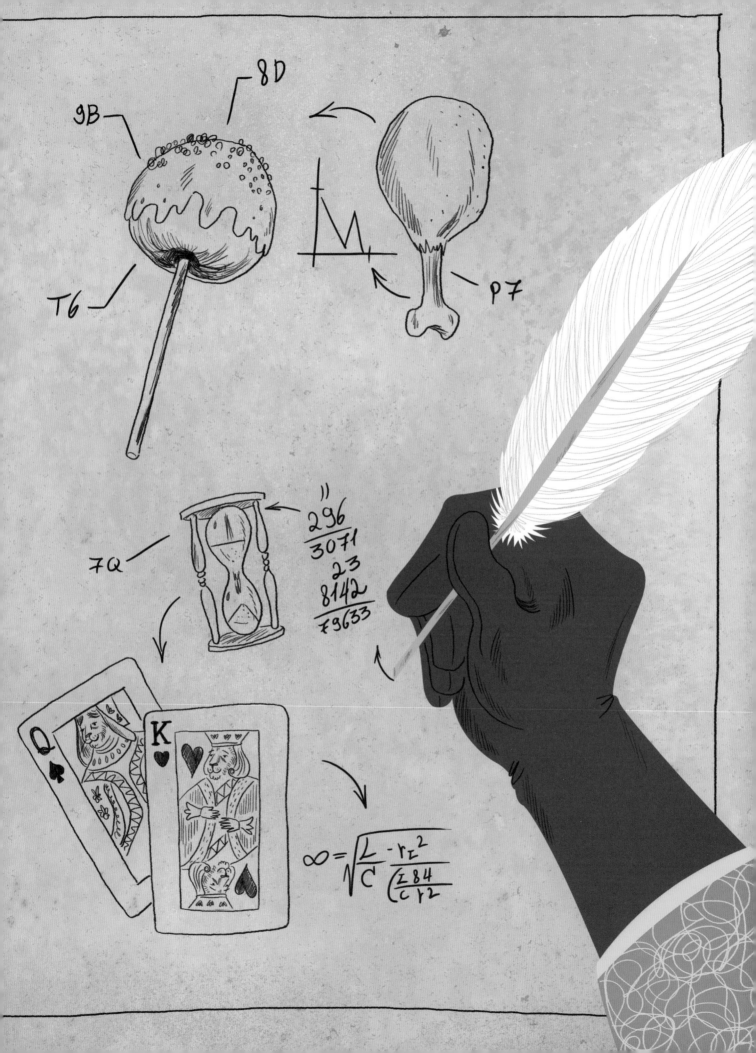

I told him that long-haired cat-boy cubs really love jokes and stories full of surprises, and that if a long-haired cat-boy cub tells a story, you have to listen to the end, even if you get a really important phone

call from work, or else it might bite you. And that they
can only drink chocolate milk and juice, because water
can make them throw up and maybe even go blind.

Habakkuk wrote
everything down
in his notebook, and
looked happy until the
sun started to set and the
notebook was almost full.
Then he said in a voice that sounded
a little sad that he had to write down
the natural habitat of the long-haired
cat-boy cub so he'd know where to
set me free, because it was
getting late.

I told him that long-haired cat-boy cubs live mostly at 17 Stampler Street, on the second floor, and that you had to lie down next to them in bed and tell them nine bedtime stories before they fell asleep. While we were still on our way, Habakkuk started telling me stories about rare animals in trouble and about daring rescues, and in the middle of the third story, I fell asleep.

When I woke up in the morning, I was back in my room, and Habakkuk's notebook was lying next to me.

Mom and Dad were in the kitchen having an argument that must have started a while ago. Mom said that Dad had acted irresponsibly, that you don't do something like that to a little boy. Dad said she was exaggerating, that I was a big, independent boy already, and she shouldn't forget that a Japanese man, a plane, and a building were also involved in what happened. When I saw that they couldn't decide by themselves whether I was a big boy or a little one, I explained to them that I wasn't a boy at all, but a long-haired cat-boy cub.

To make everything clear, I showed them Habakkuk's notebook. And since then, whenever Dad and I spend time together, he checks it to be sure he's raising me right.

A TRIANGLE SQUARE BOOK FOR YOUNG READERS

published by

SEVEN STORIES PRESS

FIRST TRIANGLE SQUARE EDITION FEBRUARY 2021

LIBRARY OF CONGRESS CATALOGING-IN-PUBLICATION DATA

NAMES: Keret, Etgar, 1967- author. | Basil, Aviel, illustrator. | Silverston, Sondra, translator.

TITLE: Long-haired cat-boy cub / Etgar Keret; illustrated by Aviel Basil; translated by Sondra Silverston.

DESCRIPTION: New York: Seven Stories Press, [2019] | Originally published in Hebrew in 2013. | Audience: Ages 4-6. | Audience: Grades K-1. |

SUMMARY: When a small boy is left by his busy father to entertain himself at the zoo, his imagination carries him to an airship, where he helps the captain put sad zoo animals back into their natural environment and teaches him about the traits of the rare long-haired cat-boy cub.

IDENTIFIERS: LCCN 2019027893 | ISBN 9781609809317 (hardcover) | ISBN 9781609809324 (ebk)

SUBJECTS: CYAC: Imagination—Fiction. | Father and child—Fiction. | Zoos—Fiction. | Animals—Fiction.

CLASSIFICATION: LCC PZ7.K4686 Lo 2019 | DDC [E]—dc23

LC record available at https://lccn.loc.gov/2019027893

Printed in China.

1 3 5 7 9 8 6 4 2

Born in Tel Aviv in 1967, ETGAR KERET is a leading voice in Israeli literature and cinema. He is the author, most recently, of the memoir *The Seven Good Years*, as well as five bestselling story collections, which have been translated into more than 40 languages. His work has appeared in *The New York Times*, *Le Monde*, *The Guardian*, *The New Yorker*, and *The Paris Review*, among other publications, and on *This American Life*, where he is a regular contributor. He has also written a number of screenplays, and *Jellyfish*, his first film as a director alongside his wife Shira Geffen, won the Caméra d'Or prize for best first feature at Cannes in 2007. In 2010 he was named a Chevalier of France's Ordre des Arts et des Lettres. Most recently, he received the 2016 Charles Bronfman Prize and, for the Italian edition of *The Seven Good Years*, the Premio Letterario Adei-Wizo.

AVIEL BASIL graduated from Shenkar College of Engineering and Design in 2011 and won the Israel Museum Award (silver medal) for his illustrations in 2012.

SONDRA SILVERSTON has translated the work of Israeli fiction writers such as Etgar Keret, Savyon Liebrecht, and Aharon Megged. Her translation of Amos Oz's *Between Friends* won the National Jewish Book Award for Fiction in 2013. Born in the United States, she has lived in Israel since 1970.